FATHER FLASHES

FATHER
flashes

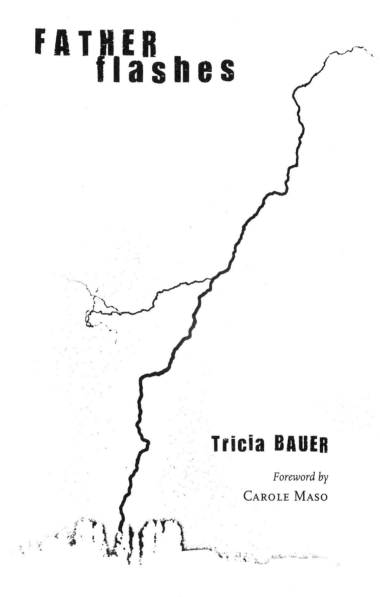

Tricia BAUER

Foreword by
CAROLE MASO

FC2

TUSCALOOSA

Published by FC2, an imprint of The University of Alabama Press,
with support provided by the Publishing Program at the University of
Houston–Victoria.

Address all editorial inquiries to: Fiction Collective Two, University of
Houston–Victoria, School of Arts and Sciences, Victoria, TX 77901-5731

Cover and book design: Lou Robinson
Typefaces: FF Scala and Pikelet
Produced and printed in the United States of America
∞
The paper on which this book is printed meets the minimum
requirements of American National Standard for Information Sciences—
Permanence of Paper for Printed Library Materials, ANSI Z39.48–1984

Library of Congress Cataloging-in-Publication Data
Bauer, Tricia, 1952–
  Father flashes / Tricia Bauer
        p. cm.
  ISBN 978-1-57366-160-7 (pbk. : alk. paper)—ISBN 978-1-57366-824-8
(electronic)
  1. Photographers—Fiction. 2. Adult children of aging parents—Fiction.
3. Alzheimer's disease—Fiction. 4. Domestic fiction.
I. Title.
PS3552.A83647F38 2010
813'.54—dc22
                                        2010017783

In memory of my father, Charles Henry Bauer, Jr.

From the porch of the house
I turned back once again
looking for my father, who had lingered,
who was still standing in the flowers,
who was that motionless muddy man,
who was that tiny figure in the rain.

—Mary Oliver

CONTENTS

FOREWORD

Suffused with tenderness, Tricia Bauer's *Father Flashes* is at once austere and lavish, simple and complex, troubling and serene. How to describe the feeling exactly? One feels in familiar territory: a parent will dim and eventually die. A child will grieve. Why then does reading *Father Flashes* feel so surprising— at once so natural and so frightening?

Perhaps it is the blank space that nearly overwhelms the text, taking shape around the fragments of father that still remain. Perhaps it is the weight of oblivion as it comes on and enters him, or the taste of it the narrator has in her mouth, or the intimations the reader gets as it takes over the pages and seems to wait.

What startles, and leaves us unmoored is that the father flashes we read are just that: brief, discrete flashes of perception or scene or memory, surrounded by empty space. Despite the child's love and attentiveness and care there is no real way to make the father whole or continuous; he can't cohere anymore. The disappearance already in progress, the man's consciousness already being taken back, when we arrive.

There's no one who can hold him, and there's no conventional narrative he can function within, no credible scaffolding that can support him. The narrative— filled with gaps and fissures and elisions, eschews the ordinary expectations; the narrator's conventional guidance and insight scarcely exist, nor does the consolation of a fully rendered character, or the arc of story, or the suspense of what will happen in the end.

At times it feels natural for the reader to attempt to put together a whole man, to fill in the blanks, to dress him up, to wish him the best—maybe he'll get better, maybe these flashes will give us something more in the end. Maybe no one will die.

Despite the wish that the past hold and that the future remain open and possible—there will be no outcome other than the one inexorably and exquisitely documented before us. *Father Flashes* takes away everything but the moment, and leaves us in its starkness—there is only this. That is what the book insists upon. There is only this, and it is more than enough, and it is everything. These moments, and the space around them and the little father flickering, engulfed in it.

"I'm carrying him, small and light as a sack of potatoes. I'm carrying him in the direction we've decided is home. He's dressed in his usual pants and jacket, socks, shoes, and hat all variations of brown.

"Without warning, at the top of the hill, he flips out of my arms and whirls down the leaf-colored incline. When he finally stops, I rush to find him, but can't for all the foliage. Furiously I dig for his shade of brown that's been swallowed up by autumn."

How will we ever hold him together?

We come to embrace what is set before us as best we can. We are asked to call up the dream of his life in some of the very same ways he does now. What we see is fleeting, partial, shadowy, incomplete, with brief flashes of lucidity. We feel the effort in just trying to keep up. When for a moment there seems to be some sort of serial chronology, some more prolonged narrative, it causes us anxiety, for we feel more keenly all we must be missing. A story about a green expanse, and a small white ball—there for a moment. What have we missed? We see in pieces, and we long for a whole that is not available anymore. And the narrative as quickly as it appears, is gone again.

"A crowd assembled to witness how stone, carefully arranged as a story, crumbles to phrases then merely sound. When the stairway was exposed I watched its ascent to our separate floors. And through the cage work of wooden bones I thought I saw my desk, his darkroom, his small corner of worth for forty-six years that he remembers not a minute of."

We feel the solitude of a human life on earth, and we are asked to consider the pact all of us who are born enter, against our wills. And the sorrow of children, who must watch those who brought us into being, and named the world for us, and showed us its ways, grow backward into forgetfulness, and then die.

Why does it shock so? I already know what happens—it happens to almost everyone: those who were once big and took care of us, now are children again. How clearly it seems a rehearsal for our own deaths, this relinquishing of the world, as we surrender a parent. Though familiar, what makes it again so keenly present, so unnerving and so strange? It is the author's art that has brought us here—that is clear enough— with heartrending precision–a precision doesn't just feel like good writing—it moves beyond that into necessity, a way to keep what we can, while we can, to hold, before oblivion encroaches and takes over.

And we, already with intimations of the end, feeling

the weight simultaneously of presence and absence; we, the not yet vanished, mesmerized, see him:

"Pressing against all that's kept him in place, he stands, shaky as if his legs are brand-new legs. He stoops just enough to aim himself in the right direction, then wobbles off down the corridor to haunt the place where he used to live. "

As the father becomes unreachable, as the space overtakes, we understand, there is nothing any of can do, but stand in awe. I think of the novel as a form—its elasticity, its capacity to create wonder and terror and beauty.

"...Here, Here, here.

"Right here," Bauer writes, "is the perfect place to witness the race to darkness." And she is right.

CAROLE MASO

PROLOGUE

All the time I wove through the browns and grays
and greens of other places, he was a farm. The solid
landscape and dependable seasons became him. Then
when I returned, each time that I came home, more of
him had been sold off.

First to go, and not really missed, was the far fallow
field, but next a meadow flecked with Queen Anne's
lace, loud with meadowlark, and thick in untrod
clover. The planted fields—wheat, alfalfa, rye—disappeared one by one. Incongruities grew up around
him—condos and condolences. The outbuildings with
their earth-encrusted tools and sleeping machinery
were broken down and carted off. Month by month we
witnessed the giving over, right up to the farmhouse
itself with its front porch sagging into a weathered
face, its steps the broken, discolored teeth.

Where is the proper place to plant a loss?

My father hasn't stepped onto a hallowed farm,
watered well with generations of nostalgia, since he
was a boy. My father has lived for forty years on a
street shorter than a good row of corn, each night the
cars growing closer along the street and plucked off
by the following morning. His mortgaged plot of dry
Kentucky Blue sits behind, an afterthought of golden
harvest.

I have made him a farm instead of the farmer that
his surname implies. A daughter takes liberties, and
time takes liberties.

I

THE SIGNS

FIRST SYMPTOMS

Their bodies give them away. Looming larger, Mother
has eaten her way beyond Father, who is shrinking to
join the metal men poised in accomplishment on his
golf trophies. They try to justify why they no longer
sleep together.

He laughs and gestures to indicate the hill shaped
in their bed she's grown so heavy. Dream after dream
he rolls into her. She scowls at how he makes himself
lighter with every trip to the toilet. "Every hour," she
says. "All night. Every hour."

My brother and I, home for a visit, do not understand the new arrangement—them in our old beds.
Just by our presence, we force them to turn back that
old landscape of nubby chenille and bleached white
sheets covering a mattress eight hours older than their
marriage. Their feet must bump the sky-blue dust
ruffle as they sigh into bed.

My brother settles upstairs, directly above me on
the double bed in the room once mine. Mother's new
domain of patterns, lengths of cotton and corduroy,
virgin wool, and synthetic silks are colorful as foreign
goods from dusty, overland hills. Some nights she
sews herself to sleep.

My brother sleeps with his new wife as I pull down
the wheat-colored blanket on a bed always his—the
single in the smaller room for the second-born. Father
claims it's inviting as a just-mown lawn.

What I hear in the next room my brother must
hear, too—Mother and Father turning and turning,

determined as animals circling a given spot before settling finally against the ground.

FAINT

Initially, Mother blamed liquor. "The booze," she said. "The booze is making him say crazy things."

In an effort to keep him from losing himself in the middle of a sentence, she diluted every golden or burnished liquid into a shade of late afternoon sunlight. Week by week the liquids paled. If she grew proud that he did not catch on, she was not relieved.

Squirrels thickened with his forgetfulness. Their plump bodies circled the house for bursts of peanuts that rained throughout each afternoon. Like overfed pets, they pulled themselves up the cement steps of the front porch for more, sometimes reaching out to tap the aluminum screen door like miniature unexpected guests.

When she had a roll of film developed, every single shot he'd taken was the same—the spot behind the kitchen door where their first dog had slept.

To both of them, the pieces of the world they knew were coming closer and closer together.

He began to notice a darkening: rats rumbling in his closet, ants dripping across his dinner, a mass of flies clapping their hands above his chest. When he ate, he put his feet on a placemat on the floor to keep the intruders at bay.

She fears something bigger than both of them fainting, and then the night taking over, pressing both of them deeper into the house, its eaves transforming into the wings of bats that beat hard against the sky.

The sky flung far out between the blackest planets set in constant atmospheric turmoil.

RETURNING HOME

My father wakes at two a.m. and sits totally dressed, complete with overcoat and woolen cap, in his small white house surrounded by the perforations of a chain-link fence that could be punched through into the earth with the right blow. Still, the worn row of other same houses would go on.

My father is waiting for someone to take him home.

My mother wakes to find him out of place, says, "Not again with the chauffeur." She demands the driver's name, his color, his sense of direction, and the amount of gas in his tank. Entering her husband's reality, she thinks she can release him from it. She never tells him his dreams have spilled out of control across the stain-resistant carpeting, the no-wax floors. She tells him never get into a car with a stranger.

He sighs and says, "The fellah should have been here by now." He promises to wait as long as he has to.

The couple next door, who have moved back into her parents' house until he gets another job, raise the volume of the TV. That laugh track scrambles up back steps and presses against the window nearest my father.

"I think I hear something," he says. Each of the walls that now frame him hold photographs he's taken of his children, his wife, night views of the city he's lived in all of his life.

My brother, who, like me, now lives elsewhere, calls for quiet, his curses soft as rumors of a mid-summer storm. Was he dreaming of children—scattered seeds in January? His eyes, as mine, must be wide with the dark.

"Kiss me goodbye," my father says from the living room. My breathing stops at what might be premonition.

We hear my mother answer, "If the guy does show up, *I'm* getting in the limousine. *You* can stay here."

Tomorrow when I take off, I'll use the only cure I know: loud music—so loud your whole body could split in half—played in a car driven so fast you can almost reach the moment many young years ago when you still believed it was possible to leave home.

THEIR REPETITIONS

He petitions the small events wheeling around him
into a dialogue with himself:
"Did you close the door?"
"Is the front door closed?"
"Did you close the front door?"
"I guess the door's closed."

—

"Did you close the door?"
Back and forth the words flow from the stutterer
trying to hold onto sounds long enough, not to be
understood, but to force them to accumulate enough
meaning that he understands himself. Then, adjust-
ing each image to the tempo of heartbeat, he pulls
detail after detail from his imagined past to hold him
here:
"Anything can get in. My mother called and called
me, so I ran up the hill to our house. My legs ached
like I don't know what. I reached into all my pockets
for the keys when this little cat brushed by me and
pushed the door right open. There were cats every-
where."
She repeats the work she has given her life to:
helplessness, need, mispronunciation guided into
meaning. Farther and farther back she goes—every
morning laying out his clothes that smell of sunshine
and wind, bending his arms toward the armholes,
moving his fingers to buttons, then buttonholes,
with a warm wet rag wiping at his face, the back of
his neck, the undersides of his feet. Eventually, she

knows, he will need diapers.

Every Saturday when I call long-distance she tells me what he's done all week, the amazing things he's said:

"How come you only have one ear?"

"What the hell is that pig doing on the clothesline?" the way once she must have reported to her own mother about my first cawing at language.

There is little difference between joy and fear when a woman is in awe of what is expected of her.

SWEET POTATOES

If she prepares Swiss steak or stuffed green peppers
or glazed Virginia ham with sliced pineapple, or any
of his other favorites, it is the sweet potatoes he asks
about, ending each meal with "You know what would
taste good? Sweet potatoes."

Because she has heard of the nutritional value of
the lumpy tubers, she contents herself with killing two
birds with one stone. At every meal he seeks the sweet
potatoes with the ardor of finding a favorite child, a
prodigal, from among the crowd of strangers. And she
does not disappoint him. He hums his satisfaction.

Once when she ignored his request, he screamed
out the dining room window, "She's starving me.
Starving me!" until she pulled it shut.

To be sure he doesn't abandon the vegetables and
meats, she presents the potato at the end of each
meal. She assumes he will grow tired of the bizarre
color—a conspiracy of sunlight, earth, and flower—
the baby-food texture, the naturally sweetened taste.
But after he has finished the potato and stares into his
plate round and white as a beached moon, he starts,
"You know what would taste good next time?"

She knows. She knows. The supermarket bin of the
things reminds her of a mass of dried, forgotten bodies. She begins to seek out the largest, thickest ones
to satisfy him. She touches the odd marred and pitted
skins, the withered tails in non-tail places. After washing them under coldest water, before setting them in

the hot oven, she stabs them hard with the prongs of a fork.

Sometimes she could almost gag when she presents the huge potato to him, slices the crusty outer layer to reveal the steamy silky inside. She deposits a pat of butter on each half, then turns away when he first takes it in. Ecstasy lasts until he swallows.

THE SETUP

The photograph he frames with his fingers, he took five years ago to finish off a roll. "What's the setup here?" he asks of the image in front of him. *He'd come home, in from startling wind after an assignment to photograph a new Jiffy Lube. His collar turned up, his hair wild as the forest undergrowth near the farm of his youth, he looked pushed through a narrow tunnel and into a still, inland sea of light. My brother, mother, and I were discussing divorces and operations and the end of daylight savings time. Often he interrupted this way and we thought nothing of it at the time.*

"One quick one," he'd said, and the three of us knew immediately that he meant to develop the film right after the shutter click.

"Hold still," he'd said. "I'll join you." The time scraped by in seconds as he made his way to the center of us and smiled. Automatically, we were together.

"Who in the hell are these people?" he now asks, as my mother brushes at the new space between them.

"You know who they are," she says defiantly, looking down through her bifocals.

He squints and says, "I think I do recognize the fellah."

"That's your son." She speaks the announcement so softly she listens to herself.

"Son, hell. He's old enough to be my father." He shakes the photograph in the air. "Just what's the setup here?"

Now she is with him, one arm on his shoulder to guide him toward the small orbit we have made of ourselves. She touches the faces of the photograph. "Son, daughter, mother, father." She looks up at nothing in particular.

"That's it?" he asks.

"It's a family," she answers the solid way she'd pronounce the obvious—"It's a meatloaf"—at dinner.

"The hell it is," he says. "Who is this old guy?" he asks, staring at the image of himself.

Then it's quiet, but for the wind that's been almost audible all along.

Often the last photographs he took in order not to waste a single frame, were afterthoughts that, over time, have ripened with more meaning than those taken with purpose. The border collie the day before she was hit by a moving van; his mother a week before a mini stroke distorted her smile; once smuggled as a baby from Canada, that tall backyard spruce before smitten by a freak hurricane, or the family before disease expressed its strength; before asides became the conversation.

EVERYTHING WE SAVE

To break up his riffs with words that jangle on against the afternoon, to jar him from that solid rhythm of nonsense, she hands him a stack of grocery coupons. He handles the torn and scissored news-print and the shinier pieces thoughtfully, as if the task can determine the rest of his day or week or life. The chore might even pull him back to his darkroom when he'd turn on the lights to compartmentalize negatives for each month's worth of photographs.

Hours later when he declares this job finished, the thin rectangles aren't assembled into her categories of paper goods, canned goods, beauty & health.... She's stunned that he sorts in another way. Stacks of twenty-cent coupons, twenty-five, fifty, one dollar litter the entire dining room table.

Everything we save will be counted out like money, she thinks. He thinks, everything we save will be of value.

TESTS

Because all this is new to him—the metallic paraphernalia clicking with the swarm of armored insects, the crisp whitened authority invading every corridor, and even the pale green hollow of the waiting room itself, because he is a Christian Scientist, mother's having her way with him.

When trouble came close—any kind of sickness or fear disrupting our lives—he retreated to the knotty pine basement to "do a little reading." *Science and Health*. Our mother scoffed, yet insisted we allow him his privacy. And privately he told us about broken bones, diseased teeth, far-sightedness, all healed with prayer that summoned God's love of harmony.

She stays with him as the doctors poke lights at different openings and punctuate his smooth loose skin with the finest needles, as they've never done before in his life. They tilt his memory this way and that. Finally, the secrets of his body, his health always entirely his own, might be revealed to her. But after these many tests, she knows no more than I do.

All those years I was a girl, which incantation worked for me—the liquids, the techniques of doctors Mother insisted I visit at the slightest change of temperature or temperament, or my father's silent, constant petitioning the perfection of the body?

HISTORY

Asked to name five cities, he recites, "Baltimore, Niagara Falls, New York. Did I say Baltimore?" And for the present president, he sticks with Roosevelt. FDR.

My father photographed that house on the Hudson with its generous stretches and layers of green. The back of the property gracefully slopes toward water, the house itself a podium to the currents of history below.

We've even seen the wheelchair, the pastel spare rooms, and his bed marked off by velvety ropes of restraint. I've snuck past "No admittance" to the upper rooms thick with aspirations.

There's a museum, too—a low brick building harboring every gesture of his administration, attesting to How He Was Loved. We've walked through the color-laden gardens, stood at his headstone, that almost-holy spot so close to the house he could have envisioned himself from nearly any window. And maybe he did.

On our last visit, despite the throngs of visitors, my father disappeared behind an outbuilding to take a piss. If once he'd captured this place on film, now he marked this territory.

DUCTS

"The tear ducts are shot," the doctor says. The man is tall and smart looking with thick-rimmed glasses, and wise enough to speak to my mother in the colloquial way that she interprets as "down to earth."

What's worn away might be a key piece of metal or polymer, not the metaphor for emotional regulation. The doctor turns to me. "It's actually the mucus membrane that's deteriorated in his eyes." He pauses, looks above my mother's head at a mounted diploma.

"Basically, there's nothing to hold back the tears," the doctor says.

If he's down to earth, I'm up in the clouds and thinking of rain.

Mother stares at Father, who complains anew that he doesn't know why in the hell he's always crying. Like a malfunctioning camera, his eyes won't focus.

She opens her arms for emphasis, one hand pointing in the direction of the doctor, the other toward me. "He wasn't the one who used them," she says.

DAYLILIES

She cuts his food into pieces the size of words. The words might be first names slashed into his memory, all now directed at Her.

"Clean plate or there's no dessert," she warns, adopting one of her roles as other.

In the evening he smiles at her. She's tired with most of her work behind her, and scanning the headlines of the newspaper. He asks, "I wonder if you'd consider going out with me." She peers over her reading for only a second before returning silently to local news.

And in the middle of the night, he comes to her, his pillow and fears in hand, and begs to sleep with her (his wife? his sister?). "Go back to bed," she admonishes, though in the morning he is next to her.

Against the foundation of their house, deep in dark beds of earth, the daylilies I once watched her space so carefully, have spread and spread, sending a confusion of roots in all directions, to make so much of the one color.

THIS DISEASE

Before it ever came close to us, I saw a woman on
TV with this disease. Secured to a door, she stayed at
ground level and watched the afternoon as if it were
her job. She held her post as the light adjusted to passing clouds, as birds came and went, as the clock ticked
loudly in the hallway.

Because she'd turned into something her husband
understood only in terms of the pets she'd once desig-
nated as *his* responsibility, he opened the can and fed
her dog food. He tied her each morning before he left
for work at the plant. And when he returned, he loved
her the way men love a dog the night before it's to be
destroyed.

In our house that night has grown longer and
longer. And this disease dissolves both memories—
her "I" altogether; his picture of the moment that
charmed his life: a dark-haired girl struck by sunlight
and determined to live by him forever.

THE QUIET ONES

All your life you go about the routine—protein after protein bobbing and drifting through a nerve cell's outer sea, repeating the buoyant rhythm of the body. When a sudden whirling not far enough below sucks this scenario into chaos, acids scratch at the protein, scorch and chew it to specks. These sticky remains propel into the brain. Sometimes scattershot darkens into a pattern. Only then do you recognize the violence inside your own body.

Everyone envisions an ultimate power, tries it on in books, mall store mirrors, the dots of the televised picture coming closer and closer together. You've seen the ones that go beyond imagining. They're on the news—"the quiet ones" who scramble to rooftops and machine gun anything shifting into their aura of fear. The descriptions surrounding their names never match what you'd expect: "He kept to himself." "Not a bit of trouble." "You should have seen his lawn. It was beautiful."

II

THE

ENTERTAINMENT

CENTER

RESTLESS

Wherever he is, he wants to go home. Even supine in his own bed of forty-five years, covers molded along his body in support of his favorite position, his mumbles reflect restlessness.

The first few times he pleaded, "I need to go home," we heard each other's breath catch, wondered which string of syllables would sum up his life. What the end would sound like, look like, none of us could guess. Well, we guessed, if silently, but we couldn't be certain of the final verbal essence—a metaphor for golf, for photography, his family... The last words might be as unexpected as the very first. My own was not "papa" or "mama," but "pocketbook," the simple click of consonants my awakening.

If his mind idles in snapshots of his youth or even a time unidentifiable to us— his children— his body has continued. Continues out of synch with who he often thinks he is.

Was he so unsettled here with us that he longs to return to his starting place, to move among his siblings, his parents who were younger than we are now? When contented, a cat pads its entire life even though the nipple is long gone. Or does he sense a momentary closure that could almost recall the workday at its end and the promise of some televised sport in the security of the house. "Home" then becomes the stand in word for anything understandable.

When I was an adolescent, still numbed with the post-operative blue of an appendectomy, I panicked that no one would come to rescue me from the hospital's unfamiliarity. I thought I saw the huge faces of my dead grandparents looking down on me through glass as surely as they must have just hours after I was born. Even my hands smelled of antiseptic. And then the eyes of my father pressed each pale green wall away and promised to take me with him.

I want to offer myself that same way, but without getting in the way of instinct. If he's mired in verbalizing the larger picture, the one beyond even death— the urge to repair and repeat to continue the process of perfecting the DNA—then I'll bend. I'll bend with a tall softening tree giving in sudden wind to make more light for everything below. I'll notice that fine shards of sunlight flash through leaves not unlike the work of a camera. I'll admit that nature doesn't pretend to hold onto any one image forever.

ADULT DAY CARE

Willingly, he lets the attendant heavy with flesh and
friendliness buckle him into the seat though, in his
driving life, he never wore a seatbelt even when pre-
caution turned to law.

His wife watches him driven off the way once she
concentrated on her children in the bus windows that
shrunk to the size of photographs. How quietly their
special voices melded with other children's, their arms
and hands dissolving to a rash of tiny good-byes.

All afternoon she avoids leaving the house and re-
gaining her old freedom to weave along the endless
stretch of food and discount stores in anticipation
of the call to tell her she's needed, that no one can
handle her husband. But the house is quiet as a held
breath without his repetitions. When she stops short,
she almost expects him to run up against her. The
living room fills with shadows; her loneliness, a sub-
stance spilled onto everything she owns.

When they return him, he doesn't speak. He opens
his mouth only to fill it with her warm candied sweet
potatoes, meat loaf, green peas. He can't remember
what he did all day. He remembers only the bus ride
home, the nauseous crawl through dense traffic and
traffic lights matching brake lights, a blur stretching
out in front of him into an entire landscape of inter-
ruption.

Her constant prompts don't help him to focus:
"Were the people nice?"
"Did you have a good time?"

"What was the food like?

"Were there games?"

"Did you dance?"

"Did you miss me?"

MESSAGE

He watches only the van coming straight for him, not the dark words along its side—*Adult Day Care*. Even the cheery red slogan on the vehicle's door—*Almost Family*—doesn't catch his attention. He seems not to notice that the woman beside him is not his wife but a nineteen-year-old focusing on her own lap-centered fist.

The place he is taken to routinely he's termed "The Entertainment Center" as if every institution is a tender joke holding back the truth. He might mean "entertainment" in the obsolete sense of employment (he goes so far off these days) because when the van delivers him back to us, he complains, "It's the same damn thing every day. I'm sick of it. The same thing," as if referring to a job. But the next morning, sometimes at five, sometimes even at four, he's ready to repeat the journey.

My father used to be a quiet man, never grumbling about work or wintertime or what little appeared on TV that pleased him. When he and my mother fought, my brother and I could hear only her voice thrown around the house, like glass juggled high above our heads, then shattering against the walls. My father answered by slamming doors, jumping into his Oldsmobile, and squealing off against the night.

In the morning, two black lines of escape in front of our house were all that remained of domestic turmoil. As I stood on one, my brother the other, we claimed a fantasy—some other-worldly creature had visited this place and left so abruptly that the unfinished message to us couldn't be deciphered.

Those infrequent fights and puzzling aftermath have prepared us for these recent departures—unexpected, often frighteningly out-of-character, and soon after, before we really comprehend what has happened, all is forgotten except for those questions—black, bold, unfinished.

FAMILY NIGHT AT THE ENTERTAINMENT CENTER

My mother and I have set him between us, in the middle of the music. Horns and organ and drums spit and push their upbeat notes all over us. He doesn't resist them or try to send his voice out over them, but turns from us and pushes back, moves toward the source of commotion. He shakes his finger at the musicians, reprimanding them for their interpretation of the evening.

After the briefest pause, the music catches in his hand just as if it's been thrown right to him. The rhythm wiggles into his fingers, along his arm and torso, setting his entire body in motion. By the next song, he's made an instrument of himself.

One by one nameless young women—aides or other old peoples' offspring—all shiny hair, tentative long legs, slick-bright layers of synthetics follow his lead and dance with him. Between songs he claps for more of the same, stomps a foot as an exclamation point.

During the meal, he alone moves on the dance floor, gestures as if directing an ocean of gentle music. Mother mentions that his dinner's getting cold.

"Enough is enough," she says, inserting her forkful of green beans flecked with almonds.

"We're going to have to carry him out," she says. What she has in mind is not what I picture.

What I envision is this: him in victory raised above all our heads but still sweating, and shaking his arms and legs in a frenzied aftershock of breaking the big fever that held him so long in such foggy clutches of forgetfulness. And someone else taking *his* picture.

ANDRÉ

"You won't believe this," my brother comes to tell me.
"I believe everything." This is why he is telling me.
He takes a breath then describes sitting next to a
woman on the airplane who greeted him by speaking
his three initials. He checked his luggage tags to see
if they had leaked his identity. But no physical letters
had betrayed him.

She knew at once that he was diabetic. During the
flight she told him that earlier he had studied biology,
but that now he had become interested in picking up
his father's work with negatives and light.

"It was wild," he says. "We were preparing to land
when she gave me her business card." He presents it
now, plain white with only black letters revealing her
name and phone number, not a single logo beaming
inspiration.

"And I went to see her."

My brother is inquisitive but procrastinates until
possibility fades to loss. So this catches me—he went.

Soon he is into it, the story of André Masséna, a
great field commander during the Napoleonic Wars.

"So, wait a minute," I protest.

He explains, "I kind of went into a trance. I remember her asking me questions that I knew the answers
to."

My brother didn't even take French in high school.
Born in an era earlier, he would have trekked into
Canada to dodge overseas duty. Now he is talking
about the Siege of Genoa.

"Wait till you hear this. This is the best part," he says, his eyes moistening.

What? A marriage? My late eighteenth century name?

He says, "The next day I went to see Dad, you know what he said?"

I shake my head at him, my brother, but I have not given up.

"I swear to God, he said this. As soon as I went into his room he said, 'Hi, André!'"

EVIDENCE

On Valentine's Day he follows instructions and folds the wide plain of red construction paper in half, as if he's just closed a door, then draws a slow curve arching into the same swerve as on that far-off day the road from work was lit with fresh snow. He'd felt the car refuse his intentions, lift above the way he knew. He didn't fight the insistent direction, but gently held on, steadying a delicate inevitability hovering above his lap, until the motor finally jerked to a halt.

Farther along that road, closer to home, he'd spotted an accident: bodies flung up against the neighborhood of his youth like lovers consumed by the afterglow. Later, the blood was hosed from a lawn the size of his own. Liquid swept down the gutters of the pale street for hours before turning pink, then clear, and freezing in place.

When he takes up the scissors to chart his own plans for a heart, he worries he is hurting the paper, the tree from which it was made. Hesitantly, he cuts along the pencil line certain he is inflicting an old pain.

"That's a beautiful heart," the aide says. "Are you going to give it to your wife?"

"My wife?" he asks.

"Here," she says, unfolding his heart, swirling its back side with glue, pressing it against a white doily with such brusque efficiency that his eyes don't have time to adjust. He sees a drop of blood on a snowflake grown out of control.

The aide instructs him to sign his creation. "So there's no confusion later on," she adds.

"What's this?" he asks of his signature on the doily. He's suddenly become left-handed.

ESCAPE

He turns from the chalky song words, each letter large as an entire paperback, from the aide's white shoes squeaking at her every turn and pause, and leaves his glass of milk, the tissues piled into a small snowy barricade in front of him, to join a woman at the front door.

"Locked," she says, then, "I'm ready to get the hell out of here." The woman is wiry, blue-eyed, *Jersey Girl* bending across the back of her vest.

"I'm ready, too," he says, looking beyond her narrow shoulders almost bent toward flight, her hair the color of the tarmac field before them. "I can jimmy it," he says but doesn't.

On their way to another door, they stop to blend into the scheduled dancing. "Don't forget," she hollers over the piano stutters.

"Forget what?"

"We have to get the hell out of here," she answers on a twirl.

"I'm warming up," he tells her, pumping his arms in the air to mimic the dance leader. When the pianist lifts her hands over her head and announces she's taking a break, the two walk down the back hallway together.

She swipes her hand across a dirty window the way he'd greet his mirror after leaving a shower. Beneath her hand the sky is such a frontier blue without a trace of cloud that he repeats her gesture all down the hall windows. Brick walls between the openings frustrate his mission for a smooth, continuous view.

When she turns the handle of an unlocked door, they stop but don't look at one another. The warm air meets them like another hand, pulling them forward and into the stillness.

"A little chilly," she announces, but he ignores her.

"We can take my car," he offers, scanning the parking lot for the olive-colored Oldsmobile he bought the day before his wedding all those decades ago. With his wife of five minutes, he'd been overwhelmed with joy at the thought of escaping every wish, every whiteness.

HERE

The moment they discovered him gone I imagine was
when he left this level altogether, turned his palms
skyward and gave up on the constant static of traffic,
the complaints of consumers, the brilliant light of the
solstice, and the paler lights of his family—each different image one more illusion on TV—and headed to
a softer plane that exists without a past or a future. A
cluster of pines in half-light and the trill of a lone bird
wooed him with, "Here, here, here."

Right here is the perfect place to witness the race to
darkness.

FAILURE

Centered in the living room, thick with smoke and conjecture, we're helpless, anxious for any reasonable string of syllables to send us back into the furrows we've made of the afternoon. In this explosion of concern, we turn inward toward each other and chip away with accusations and blame.

Somewhere beyond our front door a man squints against the metallic hum of traffic mixed with insect swoon and midday humidity. This is my father. We think he's lost among the losses of thousands of strangers—their stalling cars and missed appointments. Their misplaced keys and pending divorces. Their routines so smoothed of unique detail they are as forgettable as an autonomic response to any slight intrusion.

Who will notice him, a walking embodiment of losses. How many will turn away, fail to acknowledge how much every one of us loses each day.

The coffee table's sprayed with coffee cups; the clock worries along. His name has been repeated like a destination enough times to become background buzz in any station or terminal.

I'm used to waiting out precise mechanical failures, always thankful to the person who can repair the delay in hundreds of people's lives with a specific part and tool to fit that part. And make them believe, if only for a minute, that one piece is the secret to everything that's gone wrong.

But the brain. No, the mind. Complex as any planet.

FAST TRAIN, FAST WATER

If he'd been traveling south on a fast train—outracing building after building of workers, the blinking between TV channels, the ripening of corn and tobacco—and it had broken through a fractured bridge railing, rushed past its usual path and into fast water, and if, on seeing the diesel-colored water press like night against the windows, he'd panicked to find light until someone pulled him through the cold oily water and delivered him, discolored and shaken to shore, he couldn't be more stunned than now, standing in the doorway to his own house.

He doesn't see his photographs of the family. He doesn't see his family. He sees only boulders in a current—forms secure in their places long before the arrival of trains, bodies to grab onto and embrace with both arms, gratefully give up his body warmth to.

GIFTS

Since he's been found, everything's coming back to me and, though they seem meant for me, things I never lost: from the Laundromat last night, a pair of size five (my size) underpants; last week a blue contact stuck to my blue sweater, and just an hour ago, a paperback of easy-to-handle home repairs hidden in my canvas tote.

I've found money in the most unlikely spots: refrigerator, glove, bird feeder... and blessings in the outstretched hands of strangers at every pause in pedestrian traffic.

I must have wished for him so hard that when he broke through that elastic epidermis of hope, all the rest came pouring through, too, all the paraphernalia that tragedy drags with it. The compensation.

III

THE LANGUAGE OF THE (NOT–SO) DEAD

THE LANGUAGE OF THE BODY

In turn, my father and I stroke a dimpled round of white across silvery-blue carpet toward a cup, open-mouthed to this unusual purpose. For the moments he approaches the ball, retrieves it, mumbles, seeds it deep in his pocket with his coins (his putter, all the while, jutting up from his body as a scant wing), I see he's confused; the color beneath our feet should be green. We should be bleached against full sun not fingered in lamplight. On a real course we could blame the sand traps, spread in waves and luring dips of false reprieve, for coming between him and where he wants to go.

I line up my intentions, gently tap the ball. "A little harder and that would have gone in," I say.

"Don't say that," he says and laughs, bending forward to hold his knees. And later, at dinner when Mother relives cooking the turkey ("I put it in at two o'clock") my father laughs so hard that tears come to his eyes.

In all the years that I have known my father, never has he been so entertained in this way. He cannot recognize the determined path that his sex has taken, driven in a high arc above all that's expected, so far beyond the actualities of the body. The body driven, then held in the swing of what has already happened. On that course, hidden in the glaring burst of natural light, the ball might never drop.

THE LANGUAGE OF RESISTANCE

Three years ago he witnessed his sister stroke off from her usual routines and then from her body like the most competitive of swimmers. How she passed all those she tried to heal and did heal with prayer. How her sweet voice forgot the order of sentences, became a scream cursing through her body, then out into her hands.

She pulled silverware from soft, tarnish-resistant pouches and threw it to the floor, set overhead copper-bottomed pans clamoring against one another, grabbed, by their blooms, violets she'd once tenderly separated from the parent plant then flung them, too, onto the pile. The odd offering growing to include books, onions, a ceramic elephant the size of a border collie, high heels, shampoo.... became her barricade.

He couldn't understand why she—the practitioner—chose plastic and metal and paper to shield herself from being pulled off this material plane.

She didn't say good-bye, she said, "Hell...shit...bastard," startling him more than if she'd stood before him naked pleading, not insisting, that everything join her side.

He finally heard himself saying, "No, no, no, no..." until it became a buzz of compliance in the background of the room where everything of use was suddenly piled into uselessness.

THE LANGUAGE OF DUPLICITY

The way a bird gathers scraps of dead things—twigs and twine and dried grasses—to make a nest to last the summer or longer, my father hoards the details of every old imagining. He's learned to select incidents from different people's lives, various time periods, from television shows, even from his dreams, elaborate, then mold them to one conclusion he's convinced of.

"After I gave the monkey the banana, he ran up a tree, and then I threw a nut that knocked the damn monkey right out of that tree. He got behind me on the front nine. I didn't notice him and when I went back to swing, I caught him across the head. They took him to the hospital.

"I think eventually he came around."

Conspiring with the way things didn't happen, he tells a story again and again to press it into his past, to change his history, to make the place where he's learned to live softer, being that much farther from the ground.

THE LANGUAGE OF ANCESTORS

Even knowing his secrets—his other wives, his age (a generation beyond our mother's)—he breathes with words and names I've never heard, and his eyes hold to a spot on the far wall to steady us crossing a bridge of thick worn rope hooked far above the world.

"There's a lot you don't know," he whispers.

Before I can open a dictionary to catch "swingle-tree" from the middle of his sentence, he explains that his father (the grandfather I never saw) hitched a team of horses, handed over the reins all the while fingering one thick black mane.

The old man speaks through my father. "Here is not safe," and spurs my father on his reluctant way over fields of August-high corn.

Suddenly my father arrives at a word never mentioned in our house—Holocaust—and cries softly.

The troubled way he rides through the emblems of other eras—sulkies and petticoats and bayonets, then solid black after the last candle of the night is blown out—astounds me.

How vast the journey.

DIALOGUE (WITH THE SELVES)

Here's where we start, A B C. "From sea to shining sea," that's the end. Oh, say can you see?

What the hell are you talking about, Charlie? What's all this C stuff?

C.C.C. Ceegar.

What's a ceegar? It's cigar, you crazy fool!

You see that nice young lady there, don't you?

That's your daughter. You can't think that about your daughter.

She sells sea shells. See you later. That's what she sees.

I'm warning you, Charlie. Don't you see? Don't you know anything?

You're the picture taker. Don't you see?

It's what you don't see.

THE EARLIEST LANGUAGE

He repeats the mistakes of the toddler next door: etter for sweater, heller for cellar, halt for salt, even when the child is not visiting, like retelling the jokes of a comedian.

Malformed words creep into his speech—early symptoms of something like measles he somehow escaped when young and that now hits him harder than it would any child. He practices staccato sentences, deliberately relearning language his own way, until my mother screams, "Now cut out this damn baby talk."

"Awk awk," he petitions her, and laughs.

By the time the child next door has learned to smooth her words into unmistakable consonants and hearty vowels, he has bent words to himself for so long that sometimes only he understands the stiff inflections of what he's just said. The child points a tiny finger at him. "Say 'father,'" she says, "not 'farther.'"

He seems to know what he needs to say. We are the ones who have a problem with it.

"Farther," he insists. "Farther, farther, farther."

SILENCE

Down the road, they say, there will be no sound. He
will have walked away from his old life, left the door
behind him open wide as the mouth of a startled body.
We will stand helpless as wildflowers on either side of
him, all the while he moves beyond us toward a far,
dawn-lit clearing. For many days after, he will open his
mouth to speak and he will be fed. Long after he's forgotten how to swallow, all of us will try to feed him.

IV

THE GARDEN ROOM

TRIP

When you trip against the curb, your forehead grazing concrete, legs jutting out from under you to kick the car wheel, the voyage begins: from adult day care to hospital, hospital to rehabilitation center, rehab to nursing home, nursing home to that early fall. Pressed past decades all the way to recess, you see a head-sized rubber ball, and a group of breathless boys stopped above you, their faces silhouetted in midday sun. Though anxious to move on, one of them hollers, "OK?" and what could be more right than one of your kind pulling you into itself?

You've long forgotten the difference between nostalgia and tragedy, don't recognize that the body you've lived inside all these years can't be depended upon, but somehow you know to travel to that moment before you ever understood beta amyloid, synapses of memory, self-disappearance, when you were the center of a tight circle of pain turned to acceptance unconditionally.

For weeks you touch that abrasion with your fingers—a boy learning to bless himself.

BLOOM

His arms and wrists bloom purple, pale green, yellow. Spring is not puncturing his body with some protective groundcover, but pointed questions of blood count, potassium, sugar level. Today he knows me and puckers for a kiss, not a blush of color showing through the tight bud of his lips. His skin is so delicate and so loose about his arms it might not last the night if left outside against the cool dark and birds readying their nests for morning.

Tiny liver spots, like bits of fall leaves, spatter his hands and neck and forehead where old age has spilled all over him. I kiss him not as a child always needy, preparing for what it would receive in return, and not with the hurried obligation of those many years when he delivered me to school. As my arms grew longer I'd have one hand on the door handle, while I bent in the opposite direction toward his poised cheek. The day I determined I was no longer a child, I said, "No more kisses."

Now he's making up for those lost kisses I was once too old to grant him. And now I give them freely, as many as he wants and instantly forgets. Our lips bloom one on the other on the other because I am of him. The kiss, such a soft replica of attachment. The moment of taking hold.

TAKING FORM

Her new choice becomes which bed at the nursing home will be his. She studies the headboards, the available spaces for his pictures and bits of personal property before selecting the one near the window.

Next she shops for a bedspread. She will know it when she sees it, and finally, after the third store, she does. It's quilted and blue to match the sky. The blanket landscaped at the foot of the bed is white and blue both.

In the evening, the view from the nursing home window features only the pea-sized stone of the parking lot, just grainy enough to be real, and reminds her of all the black and white photographs he spent his life taking and developing in darkness. Never once did he photograph in color. First married, she watched him letting in the light, cupping his hands beneath the beam, above the squared off paper, shiny white. He stressed the important spots, which were the faces, brought out shadows, and later when the paper was submersed, an image began to take form.

For years, he watched her turn down the cover on their bed, smooth the white places where they would dream all night.

QUILT

When she made quilts, she wasn't thinking of passing
on the memories of a sister's blouse; his favorite shirt
worn for the first baseball game with his son; her own
soft flowered lap where he rested his hand; the corner
of the bib of the baby that became a daughter. She
wasn't out to decide what got inherited by the memory. The cloth patterns of squares, triangles, trapezoids,
and fans, stars within stars, weren't meant to stand in
for genetic traits. They were simply part of what was
called Making Do With What Was At Hand.

Now with her eyes failing, she's bought—not
made—a quilt for his new bed. She thinks of all those
old pieces saved from different wholes. She thinks of
his mind.

If she still had all the old quilts once worked into
comfort, which pattern would fit him now:

Birds in Flight
Castle in Air
Attic Window
Crossed Roads
Hourglasses
Noon Light
Moon Over Mountain
Return of the Swallows?

DINNER

When my mother finally admits that her husband is safe inside the Garden Room, my brother and I take her to dinner. We suggest wine, but she says, "I'll stick with Coke."

The crab cakes are dense with lumps of the beloved meat. She doesn't resist them as not delicious as her own, but only suggests a touch more of Old Bay seasoning. "Never trust a recipe that calls for onion with crab," she advises, though not for the first time. Onion, she is certain, is too strong for the delicate shellfish. This is wisdom I can believe.

The food relaxes her enough to admit, "Boy, oh boy, I feel like I've been let out of a mental institution." She is feeling the freedom of not having to interpret, excuse, avoid, repeat. Most of all repeat. But, by habit, she does it anyway. In truth, she wants to get another laugh. "I feel like I've been locked away for years in a crazy house."

We can't stop talking about him.

Our mother has found money, tens and twenties tucked into the small tan envelopes that organized his negatives. She says she's found a hundred and twenty but isn't done looking.

I tell them the last time I talked to him he asked if my husband was coming down to see him, too. I had arrived by plane. "He's going to drive," I answered, explaining that we'd then drive home together.

"Die?" my father asked.

"No, drive," I repeated.

"Glad I got that straight," my father said.

Mother admits to removing the fifty some rubber bands "protecting" his wallet, and finally harvesting all the pale yellow Post-it notes stuck throughout the rooms of her house, the ones announcing "Hot" or "Don't move this" and my favorite, the one on the phone that read, "Do not call your sister Bessie. She's dead." "Dead" was underlined three times.

"What now?" my brother asks. He and I have discussed her own future, his offer to move back into her house.

"Dessert," she answers. "I could go for that coconut cream pie."

HALLOWEEN

Today my father is a doctor. In his whitest clothes he glides past the other patients—Minnie Mouse and Goofy, a gregarious witch, Nixon, a cluster of ghosts, a frail angel. He doesn't pause to examine the people disguised around him. He doesn't see them, doesn't order medications or examine imaginary X-rays. Instead, he grips the armrests of his wheelchair, and, to the astonishment of every aide, pulls himself forward and up with the strength of his former self.

Pressing against all that's kept him in place, he stands, shaky as if his legs are brand-new legs. He centers himself to a far wall as if he's framing a picture he is about to take. He stoops just enough to aim himself in the right direction, then wobbles off down the corridor to haunt the place where he used to live.

DISTANCE

No matter where I am, he is there. If I'm in the grocery store picking through packages of frozen meat parts that bear no resemblance to the animals they once were, he's staring at the faint walls of his corridor or holding the handrail that runs between dead ends. That space they name The Garden Room.

Twice a week my mother stops by to pick up his dirty clothes. Sometimes—in order not to interrupt a rare good mood—she leaves without greeting him the clandestine way young mothers replace tiny lost teeth with coins. Their children sleeping off protection. And she drives home having learned what she never knew with her own children, what I've always known—when it's best to be distant.

Still, no matter where I am, if I'm innocently pushing my purchases to the cash register, I hear him asking, "What do I put this on?" to a teaspoon of sugar. Or, "I used to play golf with that fellah," pointing at a televised Walter Cronkite.

Before long, I hear him giving my name away to every attendant with long dark hair.

EFFACED

During the war, even in America, they worried. Some moved away, sheared their names of implications, left their histories meticulously folded in drawers behind them, all their possessions flattened to the pages of a book. They made a secret of themselves, didn't even wink among themselves within their conspiracy of fear.

So you're preparing for effacement. Your turning away from your history has turned, finally, against your body. You've destroyed all records, truly forgotten everything you ever were—even ten minutes ago. You're about to leave this life clean as a teardrop in a clear, deep lake.

In what seems like seconds, survival becomes mission for a lifetime. What began as a sound you denied answer to, thickened and tightened into a wish that has never betrayed you.

Even now you won't give me names.

HANDS

Christmas disrupts his smooth days, their slow gloss of meals and washing and drifting down the wheelchair-lined hallway, so unlike a path of water with the secret energy beneath. He holds up his hands not to receive, but to stop the evergreen, the commingling of colors and wrapping paper, the tiny twinkling lights that won't be blown out.

Once at Christmas and birthdays he put money in my hands to buy gifts for Mother, but now he doesn't understand "gift." He never knew what it meant to me the day he held my child hands and said, "These are hands that can remember things." He guessed— a piano player, an artist. And he stared, amazed that they had come of him.

This afternoon, my mother will stuff the holiday bird, far too big for the two of us and recall, once again, the earliest signs of his disappearance—when he didn't know the difference between turkey and chicken breast. When she could fool him. I realized there was no cure about a year later—the day he took my hand and guided it to the valley of himself to mean a body trying desperately to rescue itself.

THE METAPHOR

He couldn't have missed the metaphor if we'd driven
to the harbor together that startling bright morning. But I faced the building alone, *The Baltimore
News-American.* The derrick. The wrecking ball—an
impenetrable core of some sun blown out and earth
bound—smiled across our common history.

With each underhanded pitch, each assault and re-
verberation, memory hung fine as dust in the air. My
first job, my father's last.

A crowd assembled to witness how stone, carefully
arranged as a story, crumbles to phrases then merely
sound. When the stairway was exposed I watched its
ascent to our separate floors. And through the cage
work of wooden bones I thought I saw my desk in
editorial, his darkroom, his small corner of worth for
forty-six years that he remembers not a minute of.

All those particles of another time were carted off,
and within months the new tarmac spread like grass
over a foundation that held so much labor for the truth.

LIFEWORK

How is it possible that he who verified me at the very beginning, before I had hands or feet, a head or heart, whose sperm traveled on faith by the order of the body headfirst into collusion, who spoke my name at the moment of his climax because he knew, he later told my mother, that they would have a daughter—calling me before I was born, before he fell for me—now doesn't know my name? Has he left his lifework so far behind he's reached a place before desire for sex, for food, even for the close dark room of the mother's body?

Or is it beyond?

Are you showing how all this matter that we live within is but an illusion? How much more I am than a name?

V

THE DREAMS WE REMEMBER

THE DREAM OF CARRYING HIM

I'm carrying him, small and light as a sack of potatoes. I'm carrying him in the direction we've decided
is home. He's dressed in his usual pants and jacket,
socks, shoes, and hat all slight variations of brown.

Without warning, at the top of the hill, he flips out
of my arms and whirls down the leaf-colored incline.
When he finally stops, I rush to find him, but can't for
all the foliage. Furiously I dig for his shade of brown
that's been swallowed up in autumn.

I discover him not below, but slightly above me.
He's holding to the under bridge with water fast
around him, loud as an audience. Swimming in after
him, I fight the determined course, muddy with its
speed. When I reach him and open my exhausted
arms for him, he asks, "Are you my bondsman?"

"Yes," I answer at once. "Yes."

Of course I have paid for his losses with words.
That is what a poet does.

THE DREAM OF ANCESTORS

It's not a relief to think that a long line of ancestors will be waiting for him in some celestial receiving line. They'll take him in, pass him along, claim his eyes and bone structure, and sense of humor. There's competition even among the dead.

A family knows secrets, can use any weakness as a weapon, twist a smile into a knife blade. Love that grows not from choice but obligation should not be trusted, and yet we trust it more.

At a point in the legacy of forced love, genetic predisposition to this disease became visible. Maybe when an early farmer unexpectedly forgot to put in his alfalfa. Then, those missed rows grew weedy and everything after was at some risk.

Mere surviving might mean eventually the family defect takes hold. My father has lived longer than anyone in his family. I am linked to his staying power.

There are all kinds of tests now. One measures the extent of pupil dilation. The farmer come in from sunlight to his dark barn; my father, hours in his darkroom; me against the machinery of an eye test and envisioning the expressions of long-dead relatives. All our eyes open to such an extent only a threadband of color circles the cornea.

DREAM OF THE SELF

In the neediest terrain, a body creates more bodies to assure itself being saved. And you make so many relationships of one person.

With all you call me, I've come to await the time when it truly won't matter if I'm sister, wife, mother, lover, daughter. I'll have become an entity apart from any one fact—the bed, the stove, the breast...

It's what we work for, to become a city of people. The challenge to the self is not to feel annihilated by another name, but enlightened with each new layer of identity. Because what comes next won't recognize the designations. We won't be called by what we do, but simply what we are.

In all these years, the texture and gesture of others *you've* acquired have worn off. The personalities you've taken in have deteriorated with matter and left you one knob of wanting self. And when you call me by each different name, somewhere you must be hoping: this one. This one. One-on-one.

Over and over, you pull the separate bits to you to help make sense of yourself, but none works on its own for more than a few seconds. You don't recognize my progress. You see me still in pieces.

THE DREAM OF PLAYING GOLF

Only golf connects him to the life he's lived. My brother asks repeatedly, "Hey, Dad, when are we going to go out and hit a few balls?" as if the game were still in him. Grinning, our father feigns a swing from his bed. Everything else we say flies beyond him, like the dimpled whiteness of other players' harder drives.

I begin to dream of playing golf with my father. Night after night I return to the course. In the dreams he is agile and strong, and shot after shot I select the correct club for him, then follow him across wide spreads of green, sand traps, and water hazards without ever understanding his love of the game. The vista is always still except for his slicing through it, and quiet but for the contact of club with ball.

Not until I open books for the interpretation of this dream does it stop. These dreams, I've discovered, mean, "You will bear a son."

THE DREAM OF CHILDREN

I never wanted a child until my father became a child himself. In loving his fingers and ears and arms within that wrapping of flesh slack enough for some other body to join him, his fine silvery hair grabbing up the light, his so blue eyes like the beginnings of baby eyes, his mouth the perfect curve of new moon south of the equator, his mouth petitioning me, "Mommy," I have learned to let go of myself.

Because in his calling me the mother, lover, sister, daughter, wife, I have winced at the pointed expectations of role, I call him, not the child, but the idea for child.

And I forgive myself for not seeing the charm in his awkward concentration on things for the last times, my irritation at his squalls naming all his needs. In telling myself, His body asks to be cared for so he can ready himself for the next step, I forgot my repulsion at the odor of shit. I denounced my belief that the old imitate rather than originate feeling.

I can love the helpless body, translate it into my own body in love with my husband's body, finally, in its surrender, made strong and precise. A jewel.

DREAM OF THE DARK

As a child I never feared the dark. The dark was my father's place. I sought out its secret instruments and chemicals intriguing as a newfound imagination; I learned to respect its solitude, to knock before entering with the merest sliver of devious light stuck to me. Even now, I love the smell of fixer, and the weighty sound of the word; slick sheets of paper; liquid sloshing back and forth in shallow pans. The slender beam of perfectly controlled light that can coax memory to a recognizable face.

After our father forgot what a camera was, my brother began taking pictures of everything. Suddenly looking through the brief opening, he centered all his efforts on capture and display: squirrels, cats, girlfriends, ex-girlfriends, trees, appliances, corners. Then he deviated.

Slightly out of focus pictures erased age lines and laugh lines. Developing his own negatives and prints, he made adjustments. Later, he photographed a torn photograph—sixty years old—of our father. The slash across forehead became the slightest scar. Our mother says you have to look for it.

My brother and I leaf through boxes of loose photographs. In more than one image, I hold my brother who is a baby. We pause at a photo of our mother waving from a convertible, parked in a spot from which three states can be seen; she's transformed into a movie star.

The handsome man caught in a backswing against the vibrant greens and shades we see as sepia and white and gray, is our father.

We're lost in the images in a pale green album: an early Navy airplane, palm trees, a man wrestling crocodiles, a ship captain's dinner party. Old glue marks the place of photographs—probably even farther from our neighborhood scenarios—ripped from the black pages. With no labels we're without clues. My brother and I mention names we've heard. We notice likenesses, exchange words like sister, aunt, wife, but we can't be sure of anyone but our father. And our father's wanting to remember these people, these places we'll never identify.

MY FAVORITE DREAM

In my dream he recognized all the people who came
to the front door—the wooden, white screen door of
my childhood. He knew the visitors by photos he'd
once taken of them. They filed in to greet him, hugged
him—old men, school children, and everyone in between. Baskets of crocuses and lengths of forsythia
graced the surface of each table.

He kissed the company, told them jokes. The house
was a flurry of friends and laughing. We laughed so
hard the door flew open to the brilliant day outside,
the fields of fallow farmland before there were sub-
urbs framed in the doorway like an old photograph.

Far meadow, polished sky, flush of sunlight.

Then the door banged shut shattering the balance
of that squared-off image, and in the moment before I
woke, no one moved. And then the air moved. I felt it.

EPILOGUE

When my father died, after his body had been burned, we stood exhausted in the funeral home, my brother, my mother, and I with only a tall vase of exotic flowers and several pictures of him propped up on the mahogany tables. We waited.

One by one they came. They came with the photographs he had once taken, offered them up as bits of the past found in the most cherished places and the most common—at their wedding, around the dining room table, at their son's bar mitzvah.

The open-mouthed smiles, forty-year-old wedding dresses, store owners' pride before their new stores, the now-dead pets, and the many stories about the pictures spread all over the room. Most of the people my brother and I had never before met.

There were more photographs, too. Hundreds of others we didn't see in frames and boxes and landfills all over the country.

The images were gray mostly, black and white, the faces hard white or ivory like the smallest chunks of bone.